Stories of Yesteryear

Horse & Buggy Days

Hitching
Tie Rail

Mounting
Pillar Steps

Woman riding on pillion
"The first rumble seat"

Written and Illustrated by
Harry H. Brown

Reluctantly abetted by
Mildred B. Brown

Stephen D. Brown
91 Paradise Lane
Halifax, MA 02338

Stories.of.Yesteryear@gmail.com

Printed in the United States of America

To my wife, Mildred,
who persevered

FOREWORD

"Stories of Yesteryear - Horse and Buggy Days" is back to delight and entertain those who are nostalgic for traditional New England life. This collection of short, amusing, informative anecdotes is fun to read and come back to again and again.

Harry Brown was one of those esteemed Yankee storytellers who kept alive the folklore and history of rural life by telling and retelling stories of everyday life. As a jack-of-all-trades, after being a chauffeur and gardener for Alla A. Libbey for over thirty years, he returned to a life of farming and became a self-taught dowser, writer, naïve illustrator and a cultural conservationist who loved nature, dowsing and studying the life of the Plymouth colony.

His family has chosen to re-issue this book as a tribute to Harry (who left us at the age of 102) in order to keep alive his timeless stories and the values of old New England community life he held so dear.

Sit back and relax as this author and storyteller takes you on a nostalgic trip into yesteryear.

Harry H. Brown
1982

PREFACE

Most of the stories are true. Many, I experienced. Others are ones passed on by friends, neighbors and relatives. The stories that occurred during colonial times were based on hand scripted papers written by Asa Tomson of Halifax, Massachusetts who died in 1747.

Interesting happenings have been recorded beginning from about 1697 when the grandson of Plymouth's Doctor Samuel Fuller of the Mayflower, settled in the inland wilderness known then as Fullertown. In 1734, Fullertown became the south part of Halifax, later known as South Halifax.

Most of the events recorded are rooted in the early part of the twentieth century. It may be hard to visualize life in the early 1900's when there were no electric lights or telephones in our town. Most changes in rural areas came about because of the work done by the Grange. Their influence finally forced the powerful public utilities to bring electricity to our town.

The United States Government provided a mail service to towns located in remote areas, which was known as Rural Free Delivery. Receiving mail was the only contact we had with local and world happenings.

To those of you who lived during this era, may these stories bring back fond memories. To all others, may you enjoy reading about the life of another, very different time.

Happy reading,

Harry H. Brown

MAP OF FULLERTOWN

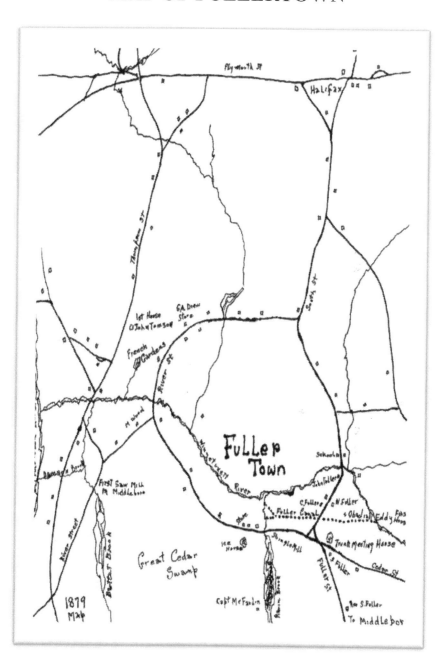

TABLE OF CONTENTS

WOLF ROCK

John Tomson was the first acknowledged settler at Halifax Massachusetts. The name Tomson was spelled as you find it in this and other stories and continued this way until changed by Reverend John Cotton at the christening of Tomson's grandson. The hearthstone of his cabin is located on Thompson Street. In the mid-1600s the Tomson family lived in the vast wilderness near the Winnetuxet River. Plymouth was the center of government and was the social, religious and trading hub of the colony. Plymouth was located thirteen miles away and was reached by traveling over narrow Indian trails. Because of the possible danger along the way, Mr. Tomson always carried his musket.

One beautiful Sunday morning in June, John Tomson followed by his two sons and Mrs. Tomson, who was carrying their six-months-old daughter, started their long walk to Plymouth to attend church services and to enjoy the social hour which followed. The family as a group had not been to Plymouth for a long time.

The walk had been very pleasant. Often a deer would cross their path, sometimes a fox or rabbit would surprise them and run past their feet. Not realizing the dangers of the wooded land, the boys were delighted by the trip, gathering woodland flowers and chewing on fresh wintergreen along the way. Sometimes they would refresh themselves at a spring-fed brook. Excitement flourished in the anticipation of seeing their friends in Plymouth.

The family was making good progress when suddenly, off in the distance the deafening howl of a wolf pack was heard. Traveling faster, they hoped to avoid the danger that was coming uncomfortably close. The howls grew louder and more threatening. There seemed to be no escape.

Mr. Thomson took quick note of his surroundings. He suddenly remembered the great rock up ahead. It stood eight feet tall with three sides shooting straight up and a narrow ridge just wide enough to climb. Not a moment too soon, the family was safely scrambling to the top of its flat surface as the wolves raged below. Quickly using the butt of his gun Mr. Tomson clubbed them away.

Later, when the sound of the pack had grown very faint, the Tom-sons descended the rock to continue their journey to the Meeting House Services singing praises to the Lord for this great rock which had been their "Rock of Salvation" (Psalm 95:1-7).

Today, Wolf Rock stands hidden in a pine grove just off Route 106 in Plympton.

In Plympton   Rte 106   John Tomson on way to Plymouth 1650 Wolf Rock

WOLF TRAP HILL

After the settlement of the Plymouth Colony, the Plymouth Court allowed those who were the "first-born" to purchase land from the Indians. In order to qualify as a "first-born", a person would have had to come on one of the first three ships arriving at Plymouth harbor, namely, the Mayflower, the Anne, or the Fortune. Formal applications were made to the Court and permission was granted when applicable.

Thousands of acres of land in Middleberry, later known as Middleboro, were purchased by twenty-six men. This land was bounded by the Plymouth Indian Trail, which led to the Nemasket River fording, thence along the Nemasket River to the Titicut River, and returned via the Winnetuxet River to the point of beginning. This was known as the Twenty-Six Men's Purchase.

One of those who was included in this Purchase was George Soule, the thirty-sixth signer of the Mayflower Compact, who lived in Duxbury. In 1690 his oldest son, James, and his brother, John, were given permission to settle on their father's Purchase. For days they tramped the region in an effort to select the best site on which to build their home. Noting the abundance of White Cedar trees in the area between Little Cedar Swamp and the Winnetuxet River they decided to build a log cabin on the knoll overlooking the river. One cold, blustery winter's day, the cabin burned to the ground. In a few days, they were hard at work building a new house.

When spring arrived, the two men worked hard clearing the land, planting their crops and erecting buildings for additional livestock. Uncannily, as soon as the land was cleared, large numbers of wolves and other predatory animals converged on the area harassing or killing domestic animals and sometimes frightening the occupants. James and John decided to dig a trap pit, which was a long, deep trench in the ground camouflaged with boughs and bushes. Once a wolf fell in, he was unable to get out. James decided they should visit the trap every other day.

One day, James found a wolf in one end of his trap and killed it. As he was about to leave, he heard a strange noise coming from the other end of the trap. Hastening to the source of the sound, he quickly removed the branches and boughs and found himself looking into the eyes of a frightened Indian boy. He quickly pulled the boy out and found that he was shaken but unhurt. During their conversation he learned that the Indian was carrying an important message from Nemasket to Plymouth and had taken a little used path to save time and had stumbled into the trap. After talking for a few minutes, he left and James watched as he disappeared around the bend.

For years the Soule brothers used this method for trapping wolves and whenever they came to the village they would delight in telling about the number of wolves they had destroyed. It was not long before neighbors referred to this area as Wolf Trap Hill.

LUKE SHORT

Many people came to the New World in the 1600's but the background of Luke Short is both interesting and unusual. He was born in Dartmouth, England in 1630, where he spent the first nineteen years of his life. During his sojourn in England, he had seen Oliver Cromwell ride through the streets and was present at the execution of Charles I in 1649. When Luke died at the age of one hundred and sixteen years old in 1746, he had lived through the reign of eight British monarchs

When he was sixteen years old, he enrolled in the British Army and served in India. One Sabbath he marched with his company to the meeting house where church services were being held. Leaving their armor outside, they sat in a group and listened to the forceful speaker, Reverend John Havel. The sermon was long and filled with admonitions. However, these compelling words, "If any man has not the Lord Jesus Christ he is not his; then how can God bless him whom the Lord has not blessed?" stayed with Luke for the remainder of his life.

After he had completed his military duty in India, he returned to England where he stayed for a period of time. Later he sailed to Marblehead, Massachusetts where he pursued a seafaring life.

The years passed and, after his marriage, he bought a farm in Middleboro where he spent the rest of his life. It is said that one day, while sitting in the shade after mowing hay, he suddenly remembered

the sermon he had heard so long ago while in India.

The verse came back to him with such force that he became a changed man and immediately sought out Reverend Pete Thatcher and joined the church.

He spent his last days with his daughter and son-in-law, Ebenezer Fuller in Fullertown, which later became known as South Halifax.

TIMBER FOR A KING

Many years ago, tall, majestic White Pine trees grew in abundance in the town of Halifax. Some were seventy-five to one hundred feet tall and when they grew along a public roadway, their branches arched over the street like an evergreen canopy. Many people were apprehensive about driving their buggies through the tunnel after dark, since, even when the moon was at its brightest, only a small amount of light would filter through the branches.

It is said that before the Revolutionary War, the King of England sent his Surveyor General or one of his deputies into the forest to direct lumbering operations. The White Pine trees that were suitable for masts for the Royal Navy were marked with a broad arrow and could not be cut or harvested even by the owner of the land. Only the King's surveyor could arrange to have them cut. After they were cut and transported to the nearest seaport, they were shipped to Portsmouth, England.

Sometimes it happened that a rebellious colonist would thwart the King's surveyor by marking many trees with the same broad arrow symbol. This caused much confusion and anger but there is no record that any colonist was brought to trial because of this act.

THE INDIAN WATCHMAN

The following happening took place during the King Philip War which occurred in 1675-1678. During this time of violence between the Indians and the white settlers, many of the people in neighboring towns fled to the Middleboro Fort for protection. When it became clear that the Middleboro Fort could no longer be protected, they moved to Plymouth for the duration of this war. After hostilities ceased, the Plymouth Court granted them permission to return to their former homesteads.

John Tomson was among those who stayed in Plymouth during the war. He and his family returned to their 6,000 acre Indian-purchase farm in the town of Halifax and built a frame house within a few rods of the site of his log cabin which had been destroyed. This frame house was unique in that the studs were faced to the middle of the sill and plates. The outer area was filled with brick and stone laid in mortar. This garrison house stood for more than 150 years.

Although peace had come to the settlers, many were still apprehensive and stories of renegade Indians in the area caused great concern. John Tomson and his nearest neighbor, Benjamin Soule, knew of an Indian named Pringle Peter who had been very friendly with them. They decided to ask Peter to come to work for them. They agreed that Peter would live with one family for two weeks and then alternate with the other family for two weeks. They approached Peter with the idea and he readily assented. He was a great help in teaching them the Indian ways and they in turn taught him many things. Each learned from the other and a happy relationship developed.

By some means, Peter always knew when there was unrest among the Indians and he would mysteriously disappear. When the Indians were peaceful again, he would just as suddenly return and continue the task he had left unfinished. This was his way of warning his friends to be on guard.

It is said that one day while conversing with John Tomson, Peter remarked, "Master, I have cocked my gun many times to kill you, but because I love you I could not."

Pringle Peter

HALIFAX FRENCH GARDENS

This story has its basis in the tragic episode made famous by the poem Evangeline written by Henry Wadsworth Longfellow. The Grand-Pre district of Arcadia, now known as Nova Scotia, had been a French settlement since 1604 but on September 5, 1775, history changed the lives of the inhabitants forever. The British fleet had entered their harbor and Lt. Col. John Winslow ordered every person in the Minos area to assemble at the Grand-Pre church. The edict was carried throughout the region and villagers commenced assembling at the church awaiting further instructions. In a relatively short time the church was jammed with anxious, apprehensive residents. As soon as the assembly had been gathered, guards were placed around the church and those in charge proceeded to the church to give their ultimatum. All persons who then lived in Grand Pre, numbering 7,000, were to board onto the waiting ships and transported to the States. In the haste and confusion of departure, friends and families were separated forever.

As the last ship was about to leave the harbor, many who were crowded on the deck watched with horror as the soldiers torched their homes and crops.

One thousand Acadians came by troopship to Boston and were relocated in surrounding towns. It is said that a large temporary prison camp was established in Halifax where the Arcadians were kept until they could be relocated.

In a handwritten document, Asa Thomson states that the Town of Halifax was responsible for six Arcadians who were garrisoned at the Thomson house under the supervision of Jacob Thomson. While living there, they planted large French gardens to the northeast of the small pond that was located on the property.

The French gardens differed from the plantings done by the col-onists in as much as they used raised beds. These raised beds could be any length but were narrow enough to allow hand cultivation from either side. This intensive gardening method allowed the ground to warm up earlier in the spring and provided improved drainage and aeration. Because of these benefits, an earlier crop of small vegetables and salad greens could be harvested.

This French garden concept is used today by home and organic gardeners and current farm magazines continue to extoll the raised bed method.

At the close of this era, the Acadians were set free. In the ensuing years, many people who had heard about these gardens came from miles around to visit the Thomson farm. Before long this area was known as French Gardens.

NATURE'S CURSE IN AN UNUSUAL CELLAR

On the corner of Main Street and Route 58 in Plympton, Massachusetts, stands a very old cellar hole. On page 164 of Eugene Wright's History of Plympton, there is a map which shows that a J. M. Mace lived here in 1879.

This is a most unusual cellar. While the foundation for central fireplaces stands in the center, the features that make this cellar unique are the iron ring hitches found along the stonewall which were probably used when the animals were brought inside for safety. Also there is a long tunnel built from the side hill to the house and another tunnel which leads from the house to the well. The latter tunnel was particularly handy during the winter months when snowfall was heavy.

Today these tunnels and iron rings can be seen in the ruins. But nature has set up a formidable barrier in the form of a thick wall of poison ivy vines. This plant, once touched, will cause anyone who dares to enter this cellar to swell, blister and itch for weeks.

UNCLE GUS LOSES HIS FISH

In the late 1800s wildlife and fish were still plentiful in the mountain foothills of Alexandria, New Hampshire. It was mid-April and the buds on the trees were just starting to open. The Trailing Arbutus, which grew in abundance at the edge of the back field, was pink and fragrant. Uncle Gus had a severe case of spring fever and felt he must go fishing. No sooner had the thought crossed his mind than he acted on it. Fetching his favorite fishing pole and gear, he laid them on the bench while he went to dig worms in the nearby garden. Everything was ready and he hurried toward his favorite fishing spot. It seemed so good to have most of the snow gone after the long, hard winter.

In a short time, he arrived at the swift-flowing river and, dropping his gear on the granite rocks, he commenced fishing. He soon caught three nice trout which he had expertly removed from the hook and tossed over his shoulder onto the ground for when the fishing became slack and he would take care of them.

Suddenly, his line zinged and went taut. He knew he had a big one and didn't want it to get away. Quickly bringing his pole up, he pulled a large, shiny, wiggling trout out of the water, over his head and onto the ground. He turned to free the hook from the trout's mouth, and, as he did so, saw the fish break loose from the hook and while still in mid-air fall into the mouth of a large bear. Uncle Gus froze. Fear gripped him like a vise. Taking note of his predicament he saw that the three trout had disappeared and the bear was busily consuming the large one he had just caught. Slowly Yankee judgment replaced fear and he continued fishing and feeding the bear.

The setting sun and lengthening shadows caused Uncle Gus to formulate a plan of escape. He knew Laura, his wife, would be worried about his long absence and would soon come to look for him. Moving slowly across the stream, still facing the bear, he climbed the small bank and stepped into the wooded area. Since the bear had been well fed, he did not seem disturbed as he watched Uncle Gus move away. When Uncle Gus felt it was safe, he quickened his step and was soon on the path leading to his back field and thence home

Aunt Laura, who was watching from the window in the kitchen, saw Gus coming across the field and went to the door to meet him. Looking at him suspiciously, she wanted to know where he had put the fish. Gus attempted to tell her but she kept interrupting. Finally, in exasperation, she exclaimed, "Do you expect me to believe that fish story?"

Uncle Gus didn't argue, considering himself extremely fortunate to have escaped from his precarious experience. Deep within himself, however, he knew it would be a very long time before he would again go to that sparkling stream in the deep woods.

THE LIVING GHOST OF FULLERTOWN

Tom "No Nose" Smith seldom came to the village store because of the stares he received from people along the way. He had retreated to a cabin near the Perkins Cemetery and his only known friends were the Horsarts who lived at Raven Brook. In November, they collected holly,  princess pine, and trailing evergreens out of which they made Christmas wreaths that were wholesaled in Boston. During the winter months, they trapped fur-bearing animals along Raven Brook.

When Smith's camp burned down one cold winter's night, he moved to the empty cabin once used by the famous Captain McFarlin. This cabin was located on high ground in the middle of Great Cedar Swamp and overlooked the long meadow bordered by Raven Brook. During deer season, many hunters told of suddenly coming face to face with "No Nose" Smith and almost at once he would disappear. This was a most unsettling experience.

Much speculation was made as to how Tom lost his nose. Rumor had it that he was suspected of being a "peeping Tom" and someone decided to find out. That someone set a window trap in an effort to catch the culprit and early one morning he was awakened by a loud scream. Jumping from his bed he found Tom Smith tightly fastened in the trap.

The "peeping Tom" story gained credence through an episode told by Rube Braddock. Rube had started his barn chores very early one morning. As he was heading for the barn, carrying his milk pail, he heard someone scream. He stopped to listen. The scream came again and it seemed to be coming from his neighbor's house. Rube dropped the milk pail and started racing across the field. Mrs. Fuller was a recent widow and thinking about this caused Rube to drive himself forward with great speed. Arriving breathlessly at the kitchen door, he pushed it open just as "No Nose" Smith jumped out the window and headed for the woods.

"No Nose" Smith was never seen in Fullertown after this and it was believed he had moved to Plympton, a neighboring town.

FIRE ALARM BELL

It is hard for us to visualize a town without a fire department, but not long ago, whenever a fire broke out in our town, the church bell was vigorously tolled. Farmers who heard the tolling bell would run from their fields, throw pails and shovels onto their wagons, hitch up their horses, and drive furiously to the church to find out where the fire was, then gallop off to give assistance. Usually, by the time they arrived at the scene, the building was engulfed in flames.

The Grange was very active in community projects and decided that there should be more than one location for tolling the bell. Perhaps it would be a good idea to put bells in different parts of the town to take care of the needs of those living there. After much discussion, it was voted upon and the Grange had a lawn party to raise money for this project. A lawn party is usually held in July on the Town Hall grounds where different tables are set up from which a variety of items are sold. Also there are contests for the children and later in the afternoon,

a barbecue. With the profits from the lawn party, the Grange bought a large bell and stand holder which was mounted on the barn of Clarence Devitt who lived at the corner of South and Hayward Streets. Whenever a fire occurred in this area, someone would rush to Devitt's barn and toll the bell.

This method of bell tolling continued until the telephone lines were installed as far as Devitt's farm. The bell was then removed and taken to the barn of Lewis Brown who lived further down the road. It was hoped that in the event of fire, Clarence Devitt would hear the tolling bell and telephone the fire department. He usually did.

✐✐✐✐✐

ANSWERED PRAYER

"More things are wrought by prayer" so thought the rain-soaked parishioners as they huddled around the pot-bellied stove in the church vestry for their weekly prayer meeting. During their three mile ride to church that evening, the gale winds from the north blew the driving rain into the front of their buggies making the ride most uncomfortable.

After talking about it, they decided that they would make the storm a matter of earnest prayer. They participated with fervor during the hymn sing and prayed in great earnest that the Lord would change the direction of the wind.

The meeting ended and the buggies were brought to the church entrance for passengers. Their prayers were answered in an unexpected way, for as they drove home in a blinding gale, they realized the wind was now blowing from the south.

FARMER BROWN GOES TO THE DENTIST

Farmer Brown had a bad tooth which was giving him much pain. One morning after breakfast, he harnessed his horse to the light wagon and drove twelve miles to Middleboro to the nearest dentist's office.

After the dentist examined his tooth, he said, "I will have to give you gas as this will be a long and painful procedure." After the tooth was removed, the doctor escorted Farmer Brown to his wagon seat, untied the horse and headed the wagon in the direction of home.

All the way home Farmer Brown, still under the influence of the gas, carried on a one-sided conversation with the imaginary dentist he thought was still with him. Three hours later, the horse arrived in the yard.

Looking out the window, Farmer Brown's wife became alarmed at seeing her husband sitting idly in the wagon. As she approached him she heard him talking to someone. Looking around to see who he was talking to, she saw no one. She then addressed him by name speaking slowly and distinctly. He turned to look at her and then released the reins. As he started to climb down he said, "Aren't you going to invite the dentist to supper?"

JOHN WYNOT TAKES A WIFE

In the early 1900s, John Wynot lived on a small farm next to the Trunk Meeting House in Fullertown. He had no family and, being lonely, made a nuisance of himself by calling on Edna, a neighbor's daughter who was not interested.

Her family came up with an idea: why not find him a wife from the Lonely Heart Column listed in the Boston paper? John could neither read nor write, so in order to solve the problem, Edna decided she would write for him. She read some of the ads to him and he decided he wanted to reply to the ad placed in the paper by a lady from Nova Scotia. Soon the two were carrying on a courtship by correspondence.

After a period of time, arrangements were made to meet the Nova Scotia lady, known as Mittie. She was to meet John at the Halifax Depot which was five miles away. The day of the meeting arrived. Edna and John, dressed in their best clothes, drove a nice pair of driving horses with a carryall wagon to meet Mittie at the station. They arrived early and waited anxiously. As Mittie stepped down from the train, John rushed to greet her. It was love at first sight.

Mittie remained in Halifax, staying on with Edna. Soon there was a wedding. Edna was maid-of-honor, and Edna's family was relieved!

TRAMPS IN THE EARLY 1900's

In the early 1900's, the railroad was prosperous and tramps rode the freights and had a society of their own. During their travels, they developed their own codes and wherever they received a good reception, a secret mark was placed by them on a gatepost or mailbox support. Halifax had a tramp house where they could not only sleep overnight but were provided with supper and breakfast. Some records show that as many as eighty tramps a year received such aid.

In theory, a tramp who was fed by you was supposed to do a chore of equal value. If the weather was inclement he usually asked permission to sleep in the barn. As a general rule, they were of good character and could be trusted. This was important because they needed the goodwill of the people if they were to travel this way again. Often there would be tramp camps near the railroad water filling station or else on a grade where the freight travel slowed enough to allow the tramps to jump on for the ride.

I expect one reason we had so many tramps was that one did not have to walk more than eight miles in any of three directions to reach a train to carry him to a city.

In the fall, when it became cold, either the tramps headed South, or as many did, would get drunk on purpose so the court would sentence them to six months at the State Farm in Bridgewater. Here they would rejoin their old buddies and plan next year's trips.

PUBLIC HORSE SHEDS

As the church membership increased in the town of Halifax, so too did the number of horse-drawn buggies and carriages standing at different angles in the church yard. During the summer months this did not pose a problem except on very rainy days when everyone wanted to be picked up at the church door. The people became concerned, however, about the lack of protection for the animals, as well as the carriages, during the winter months.

They, therefore, brought the subject up at their monthly church meeting and voted to build a partitioned shed to house the horses and vehicles.

A long shed was erected in back of the church which was opened to the south. At the west end of the shed was a two compartment one-hole each outhouse for restroom conveniences. At this time there were no facilities in town buildings.

Later, when the Halifax Grange was organized, there was an even a greater need for more horse sheds, so a large enclosed shed was built at the rear of the present town parking area. This large shed was used until the automobile became prevalent.

It was then sold to the town and used by the highway department. Many years later, a new town highway building was erected on Hemlock Lane. As the sheds had become obsolete and were in a sad state of disrepair, they were demolished.

THE SPONTANEOUS RACE

Two neighbors had a strong dislike for each other. One day they happened to drive their buggies into the street at about the same time and they were going in the same direction. Each was determined that the other would not be first. They raced along and were soon riding side by side. As they approached the bridge, each driver thought that the other would give in at the last moment. However, this did not happen and they found their buggies locking wheels and the side bridge guard rails at the same time. The buggies struck with such force that one neighbor was thrown over the guardrail into the river. Simultaneously his horse became spooked and ran away with a broken harness.

The other neighbor's horse was drawn to a stop because of a broken buggy wheel. The driver jumped out of his wagon and went to the aid of his neighbor in the water. He reached his hand and, as they looked at one another, they started to grin sheepishly, then clapping one another on the shoulder, they declared it an even race.

EDMUND CHURCHILL

Edmund Churchill had grown up as a distant neighbor of Eugene Wright, the author of Tales of Old Plympton. In his boyhood, he tells he rowed with his father from Monponsett Lake, up the Snake River past the Indian Trail Crossing to the corner of Furnace and Elm Streets to Thomas Croade's store.

Edmund knew a lot about the history of Halifax and loved to tell stories about it at the church meetings which he faithfully attended. He lived in a small house across the street from Police Chief Waterman. He walked to church every Sunday and, during the week, he helped Nettie Thomas and her father, who was the minister of the local church as well as town librarian.

Edmund had worked for years at the Old Colony Nursery which was destroyed by fire in 1890. This nursery was the site Alla A. Libbey purchased in order to re-erect the former Half Way Tavern which had been located on the Old Stage Road outside of Brunswick, Maine.

Edmund Churchill's favorite hymn was "Come to the Church in the Wildwood" and he always loved to sing, "Oh, come, come, come, come to the church by the wildwood."

He lived with Mrs. Florence Hayward when his health was failing and, when he died, Miss Zillah Baker, the Sunday School Superintendent, raised the money to buy a fitting stone as a memorial to him. This was placed at his burial place in the old cemetery on Plymouth Street near Richmond Park.

RALPH'S WINTER PALS

Ralph, an affable bachelor, lived with his mother in the small village of Brownville in northern Maine. Here the winters are bitter with intense cold and deep snow which last until late May. Ralph did odd jobs besides acting as town librarian and superintendent of the local cemetery. In the summer, he took great pride in keeping the cemetery grounds neat and orderly. But in the winter the snow often piled up eight or more feet above the tombs so bodies cannot be interred. For this reason, many people requested cremation. They asked that their urn be given to Ralph who often had talked with them about their wishes.

When an urn was given to Ralph during the winter season, he placed it under his bed until late spring. At the time of this story, Ralph had three urns under his bed and referred to each by name. In fact, very often his friends would ask him about his winter pals who were residing beneath his bed. Ralph would reply that Ben, Charlie and Jack were just fine and easy to get along with.

When late spring came and the snow had disappeared, Ralph's mission began. Charlie had talked with Ralph at great length about what he wanted done with his ashes, so Ralph decided to comply with his wishes first. Taking the urn he went to Lake Ebeeme where he placed it in his boat. Starting the motor, he took a ride out to the middle of the lake where he and Charlie had spent so many happy hours fishing and boating. As he sat in the anchored boat, he thought fondly about Charlie, remembering the times he visited him at his lake cottage and how they often watched a moose grazing in the rushes on the shore of the lake.

As he recalled their many fishing trips, he remembered one particular morning when they had left earlier than usual. After an especially good catch, they had motored to the nearest shore where they cleaned and washed the fish on a nearby flat rock. As they motored away, they looked back to see a family of raccoons cleaning up the remains. It was Charlie's wish that his ashes be dropped over board in the fashion of a sea burial. This Ralph did as he bid goodbye to his first winter pal.

Ralph's next project was to climb to the top of Mt. Tom with Ben's urn. Ben had climbed Mt. Tom many times. He loved watching the beautiful sunsets over Lake Ebeeme which stretched like a jewel below him, framed by the purple, hazy mountains beyond. Taking the hand-drawn map from his pocket, Ralph had no trouble finding the large rock beside which he was to bury the urn. As he bid farewell to another friend, he watched the sun set behind the mountain range.

When the lilacs were in full bloom, Ralph rode with his third winter pal to a pleasant farmhouse just a few miles south of his place. Ralph had often driven out to Jack's place and had known most of the family members. As Ralph drove into the now deserted driveway, he looked fondly about, letting his eyes rest on the large green oak tree that had been planted the day Jack's father was born. Jack and his friends had often played beneath its spreading branches. In times past, the air had been full of talk and happy laughter as friends and neighbors gathered for barbecues and a game of softball. After college, Jack had come home to be married beneath this beautiful oak tree. Countless memories flooded Ralph's mind as he lovingly buried the urn beneath this tall, stately tree.

Ralph drove home slowly. His task was done and he was glad to have had a part in carrying out the wishes of three very dear friends.

THE GIANT TURTLE

It was a cloudy day in early May. The weather had been foggy and wet for several days and about the only thing one could do was to go fishing. Gene Goodwin and Charlie Chamberlain got their gear together and walked down to the bridge on South Street which crosses the Winnetuxet River. Baiting their hooks with worms, they dropped their lines into the river.

The fish were biting well and they had caught a few perch, shiners and an occasional horned pout. Tired of standing, they sat on the top rail and began daydreaming about the delicious fish fry to come and watching the bobbers on their lines turning and twisting with the current.

Suddenly Charlie's line went taut and was pulled downstream so hard and fast that Charlie lost his balance. He fell into the river with a great splash, still holding his line. Gene quickly scrambled down the river bank and helped Charlie get ashore. While pulling in the line they saw a great head appear on the river's surface and they stared in consternation at what appeared to be the largest water snake they had ever seen. Cautiously, they continued to pull in the line watching with some apprehension. Then, to their great surprise, two great claws broke the surface the water. They knew then that they had hooked a very large turtle.

The mailman, driving his horse and mail wagon across the bridge, heard their shouts and decided to investigate. Hitching his horse, he quickly went to their aid.

Together, Jean, Charlie and the mailman, dragged the turtle onto level ground. They stood exclaiming about its gigantic size and ferocity. After a while the mailman promised to ask Charlie's folks to return to the bridge with a horse and wagon.

Soon the Chamberlains arrived, and the turtle was taken back to the homestead where it was put in a pen.

As the mailman continued his route, he told everyone who was waiting at their box about the turtle, just as he always told them any other local gossip that he had picked up. The news spread like wildfire and soon the Chamberlain yard was full of people who came to view and comment about the great turtle. After the newness wore off, a travelling salesman paid cash for the turtle and sold it to a Chinese restaurant in Boston where Gene and Charlie's novelty became nothing more than turtle soup.

THE FENCE VIEWERS

Long ago the Halifax Selectmen appointed three Fence Viewers to represent them in settling any dispute that might arise between two neighbors over land boundaries. Such was the case when Mr. Smith of South Street and his neighbor, Mr. Shroder, appeared before them and requested the services of the appointed Fence Viewers. A time and date was set up.

Three weeks later, the Fence Viewers drove into the yard of Mr. Schroder and, after talking with Mr. Schroder and Mr. Smith and viewing the survey map with them, they set off to walk over the disputed area. While tramping the lines, they all commented on a large oak tree that grew on the disputed boundary.

When they returned to the Schroder home they were invited into the house where Mata, his attractive daughter, served them home made doughnuts and coffee. The problem was discussed with all parties and everyone felt satisfied with their findings.

After leaving the Schroder house, the three Fence Viewers began to discuss the boundary lines. One of the men said, "That was as beautiful a trunk as I've seen in a long while."

The second Fence Viewer commented, "I agree. Weren't the limbs superb?"

The third Fence Viewer, looking incredulous, asked, "Are you fellows talking about the beautiful oak or Mata Schroder?"

THE HIT THAT MISSED

Miss Haliday had taught in the Central School for many years and was greatly respected by both the children and their parents. The school day had been especially trying. A group of the older boys had been in some kind of trouble all day and one of them had finally succeeded in getting to her. She moved quickly down the aisle and, taking the culprit by the upper arm, brought him to the front of the room for punishment. Unknown to her, he had rubbed his hands well with rosin and armed with an arrogant confidence he strutted unhesitatingly beside her.

Rosin is a hard amber substance which usually comes from fir or pine trees. It is yellowish or dark brown and is usually translucent. Many believed that if you rubbed it on your hands it would not hurt when you were struck by either a stick or a strap.

The boy held out his hand and Miss Haliday, looking very severe, proceeded to vent her frustration. But she soon became exasperated when the boy appeared to be enjoying all of the attention he was getting. Swinging the strap extra hard, she was amazed when he suddenly pulled his hand away and the descending strap struck her leg with a sharp painful blow. She doubled over to hide the tears that stung her eyes. Quickly dismissing the offender, she limped to her desk and continued to teach the lesson as if nothing had happened.

For the rest of the day the class was the ultimate in decorum. They had empathy for their favorite teacher who was continually thwarted by the antics of this group of boys.

THE BLUE MILITIA

Perhaps there had not been so much excitement in Fullertown since the Indians camped on Gravel Hill. Now the Blue Militia had come to set up their encampment on the same site, and engage in a series of maneuvers which many local citizens referred to as the "mock war between the Blues and the Reds."

It was a cool, clear Friday afternoon. My brother and I were working in the garden, when, off in the distance, we heard the sound of marching feet. Dropping our hoes, we raced across the field to the side of the road where we waited breathlessly.

At last they came into view, mounted soldiers with flags held by staff holders in their saddles. These were followed by the cavalry and horse-drawn artillery. There was a break for a little while and then came the flag bearers, flanked by drummer boys, who were followed by the foot soldiers. These soldiers wore blue uniforms with decorations indicating rank and carried their knapsacks and bedrolls on their backs and a rifle on their shoulders. This was a beautiful sight. Lastly, we heard the chucking sound of the supply wagons drawn by a matched team of horses which moved in smooth rhythm up the dusty road.

We had the feeling that this was a special parade just for us. Even the horses seemed to lift their hooves a little higher as they pranced before the small audience and the marching soldiers had a new spring to their step. Up the road they marched and then moved onto a large gravel field where the Indians had camped years and years ago. On command, they fell out of formation and started to set up camp.

To the left side were the chuck and water wagons and then the command post and officers tents. Along the rear of the field, soldiers were setting up their rows of tents and we could hear them pounding in the tent pegs and their rifles were stacked wigwam style in front of their tents.

To the right of the field, the artillery and supply wagons were lined in rows and the horses were hitched to tie lines in their corrals in the rear. Finally, mess call was sounded and the soldiers lined up to be served and fell out in groups to eat.

28

As darkness descended, the campfires were lit and as they glowed with flickering flames, the soldiers sat around them to keep warm. Some joined in campfire songs to the plaintive music of the harmonicas. At last, taps was sounded and all was still. The only sound that was heard was the call of a whip-poor-will or perhaps the neigh of a horse.

The next morning I heard the reveille call. The camp became a beehive of activity as the men prepared for their maneuvers which were usually within one day's riding distance from their camp.

In those days, soldiers were allowed some freedom. Some would pay a farmer for the privilege of a "soft sleep" in his barn. Others would pay a farmer's wife for a home-cooked meal while the children would be on guard so they would not be caught off duty. Still others would buy home-cooked food and cold drinks. Farm families took advantage of this to bring in extra income. However, they did have to be careful of their water supply because, with so many soldiers, they would soon pump the well dry. One farmer would have no part of it and put a bee hive on his well to protect it.

After a while the maneuvers were finished and this location and campground became a field again. But all of those who witnessed this colorful event will remember it for all time.

THE CHAMBERLAINS

Every small town has its local characters and our town was no exception. The Chamberlain family consisted of a father, mother, two grown sons named Charles and Horace, and a dozen cats with runny eyes. One day they drove into the yard of an abutting farm with their wagonload of belongings and became our next door neighbors.

Father Chamberlain did odd jobs as well as took care of his farm and animals. He loved flowers and particularly roses which covered the trellises of his gray shingled house with a blaze of color every June.

As children, we loved to watch Horace work with his pair of oxen. Using his goad stick plus a few unprintable words, Horace used the oxen on the farm and to haul cedar, pine, or hardwood from boggy areas to a loading location where horse-drawn teams could cart the wood to market. Then, too, the oxen were especially good when used for pulling stumps and clearing land.

During the wood cutting season, Charlie and his brother lived in a portable shack in Great Cedar Swamp with a group of other wood-cutters. Off-season, Charlie would live at home, cut meadow hay and help Horace with his oxen.

Horace and Charlie were constantly arguing, and when things got too bad, Charlie would move back to his Cedar Swamp shack until he cooled off. Then he would come home again to work with Horace and go fishing on rainy days.

The years passed. Father Chamberlain became very ill and was confined to his bed with a high fever. One morning at daybreak, Ed Hayward happened to look out of his window and in consternation saw a staggering figure moving across his cornfield. He raced across the yard and into the field to find Father Chamberlain dragging some of the clothes from the scarecrow and stopping occasionally in a vain effort to get them on. Ed supported him to his house where he got some warm clothes and blankets. Later he took Father Chamberlain home in his wagon. He never recovered, and died a few days later.

The responsibility for running the farm now shifted to Charlie and Horace. In the course of time, they decided to shingle the roof as it was leaking badly. They put up a staging, set the shingles in bundles on it, and proceeded to tear off the old shingles. As they were on the staging they got into a violent argument. Horace swung his hammer at Charlie who ducked just as it struck the stage bracing with a great thud. Instantly the staging, with Horace, Charlie and the bundles of shingles, came crashing to the ground. Following this was a great silence which lasted for a moment and then exploded into a thunderous stream of unbridled language. Horace walked slowly toward the house and Charlie headed for the river to go fishing.

Try as they might, Horace and Charlie just could not get along together. One day, Charlie moved into his one room shack located near the Winnetuxet River. Living alone was pretty monotonous and when John, the backpacked peddler, visited him, he told him how lonesome he felt. It was not long after this that a stout woman with two boys moved in with Charlie. However, Charlie soon learned that he couldn't cut enough wood to pay for their food and clothing so he went to work in East Bridgewater.

In the meantime, Mrs. Chamberlain was having her problems. The days were long and uneventful. The work on the farm and home repairs were piling up. She had to think of a way to solve this dilemma. While doing dishes one day, she remembered that at one time she had been quite attractive. If she could find her photo album perhaps she could come up with a good idea. She found the album and in it was an excellent picture of herself. As she studied the photo, mentally checking off her attributes, she decided to place an ad in the Lonely Hearts column in a Boston paper and enclose this picture together with a short write-up. Immediately she wrote up the article about herself, enclosed the picture, and, together with the usual fee, mailed it to the newspaper.

In the meantime, she talked with Horace about what she had done. Horace thought about it and the more he considered the advantages, the better he liked the idea. He would not only have a stepfather, who would probably have some money which could be used to repair the place, he would also have someone to help with the chores. Thinking about all of this, Horace readily acquiesced.

31

The ad was so good that the response on weekends kept the liveryman happy at Halifax Depot. The gentlemen who were interested took the train out of Boston and upon arriving at the depot would hire the liveryman, who worked for Ed Dutton, the station master, to drive them to Chamberlain's, a distance of five miles. If the gentleman arrived in June, he would be impressed with the gray shingled house covered with rambler roses and the flower gardens beyond. He paid the liveryman for the trip and dismissed him even before going to the door.

He had seen the curtain fall into place as he came up the walk so he knocked gently on the door. The door was opened by an excited, giggling old lady. The prospective groom did not have many choices. He would either grin and bear it or walk the five miles back to the depot. Then again, perhaps this woman was the mother of the young girl in the picture. When he asked about the photo in the paper, she told him that it was a picture of herself when she was young. Hesitatingly he entered the room and when he saw the table legs set in cans of kerosene to keep away the crawling things and the greasy chairs beneath, he realized he had been duped.

He sat by the window contemplating his next move while she rambled on and on. He tried to weigh the advantages of fresh air, home-grown vegetables and a house in the country compared with the life he was presently enjoying in the city.

Mrs. Chamberlain was hurrying around preparing a delicious supper, and, as it cooked on the stove, the gentleman realized that he was very hungry. Mrs. Chamberlain called Horace in her gruff, loud voice and when he came into the kitchen with his dirty work clothes, he stood staring at the visitor. He sat down without washing and just as the visitor was about to lift his fork, he glanced up to see Horace wiping his runny nose with the sleeve of his shirt. He immediately had lost his appetite.

After supper he was shown around the farm and realized it had great possibilities. Later, he was shown to the master bedroom where he spent a most restless night. Arising very early the following morning, he thanked Mrs. Chamberlain for her hospitality and walked five miles to the depot to get a train for Boston.

Every weekend until cold weather, a prospective groom would show up at the Chamberlains' and there were all kinds of reactions. Most of them would stick it out overnight and occasionally one would stay for a few days. Whether it was the excitement or something else, Mrs. Chamberlain did not live through the winter. Horace went to a rest home. The town officials took care of the cats and then sold the livestock. Eventually the town officials sold the farm.

THE GIFTS

My grandfather owned a large shipyard in Salem where they built clipper ships and whaling ships. He had not had a vacation for many years and decided he needed a change. One day, he took a trading trip to Jamaica on one of his own sailing vessels. He was so intrigued with this beautiful island that he wanted to bring something exotic back to his wife. After visiting many shops, he finally decided to buy an unusual parrot which he carried gingerly to his quarters on the ship.

The holds of the ship were fully loaded and he decided he would stroll once more along the streets of this lovely island. While walking along, he came across a Jamaican woman cruelly beating a young boy. He interceded and, in the course of the conversation, she agreed to trade her son for a barrel of flour.

My grandfather took the boy by the hand and together they walked to where the ship was anchored. As they waited to board the ship, my grandfather stooped down, and putting his arms around the boy's shoulders said, "Manuel, I will try very hard to make you happy." The boy smiled shyly and putting his small hand into the big hand of the older man, they went on deck where Manuel was introduced to the crew.

Manuel shared my grandfather's quarters with the parrot. Manuel, with the parrot on his shoulder, was often seen by his shipmates who enjoyed having the young lad aboard.

They encountered no unusual seas while sailing to Salem. Manuel had learned to love the sea. He watched the white sails strain in the wind and was exhilarated by the ship's movement beneath his feet. "Someday," he promised himself, "I will become a sailor." His reverie was suddenly broken by the tremendous activity which was taking place on the ship. As he watched, he saw the prow point toward land, and knew that soon they would be arriving at Salem Harbor. He raced forward to see this new land which was to be his home.

In the meantime, Annabel, my grandfather's wife, had been watching from the widow's walk on her house and had seen the ship as it came into the harbor. She flew down the steps and out of the door and raced to the dock to greet her husband. She was greatly enraptured by the parrot and was surrounded by interested friends who made all sorts of comments. It was not long after this, however, that she gave the parrot away because of its foul language.

Manual stayed with my grandparents after his arrival in Salem and loved to go down to the shipyard to watch the activities there. My grandfather knew a couple who wanted a son and after they had met Manuel they loved him at first sight. The feeling was mutual and it was not long after this that they adopted him. He often came to visit my grandfather's home and grew up to be a fine citizen.

Hattie was built and owned by my grandfather, Joshua.

HIGH SOCIETY

This story took place in a village that was miles away from the nearest city. Bill liked living here but was concerned that there were so few young women of marriageable age. He did find Gladys very attractive, but still, she was not the one he wished to marry.

However, Gladys's father, who owned a small factory and was the only one in the village who provided employment, had other ideas. Bill had worked for him for two years, and had just received a promotion. One day Bill was called to the office and was told that it was about time that he "cut bait or fish." In other words, Bill was being told to either become engaged to Gladys or leave town. Bill was silent after this ultimatum, and really didn't know how to reply. The older man observed his distress and suggested that Bill think about it. He suggested that Bill come to the house a week from Saturday to have supper with the family and meet a few close relatives.

After work that night Bill frantically sought the advice of his best friend, Paul. They discussed the matter for some time. Paul suddenly had what he thought was a great idea. He said to Bill, "I have an easy solution. Go to the supper and put on your worst table manners. Believe me, that will get you off the hook fast and besides, you will be able to keep your job." It sounded terrific and so Bill took Paul's advice.

The fateful day arrived. Bill rang the front doorbell and was greeted by Gladys, who proudly introduced him to their guests. Everyone engaged in small talk until they were called to the large dining room table. The meal was delicious but Bill did everything wrong that he could think of as far as table manners were concerned. As the meal continued, he couldn't think of anything else to do, so in desperation he started eating with his fingers and chewing with his mouth open. Suddenly, everyone at the table stopped talking and looked at one another. Someone said, "By Jove, he's one of us!" Immediately dropping their company manners, they started using their fingers and really enjoyed themselves. Bill stared in consternation, for he knew now that he was really hooked. Or, was he?

BOUNTY

When the early settlers started clearing the vast wilderness, they found that the wild animals and birds were extremely destructive. The birds would swoop down like vultures, destroying their crops. The wild animals in great numbers would destroy or harass their domestic animals. Also their gardens were trampled and eaten by the abundance of deer which populated the area. It was most discouraging.

The settlers finally offered the Indians a bounty for each wolf killed. The fee was paid upon proof of having destroyed the animal. Working with their neighbors, they also constructed deep pit traps for the larger animals.

Later on, in desperation, the settlers appeared before the Board of Selectmen and petitioned their support to rid the town of vermin. The Selectmen agreed that something should be done.

In March 1738 at the Halifax Town Meeting, it was voted that a bounty would be paid on specific animals. Twenty shillings were offered for a wildcat over one year old and ten shillings for one under one year. Because certain birds caused great destruction by pulling up the corn seed, the Town paid three pence a head. Again in March 1740, the Town voted that every household should kill, before June first, six blackbirds, six jays and six squirrels, and their heads should be brought to the Town Treasurer who would then pay two shillings for each head presented.

By 1900, the town of Halifax being advanced in age and civilized to a remarkable degree, no longer issued bounties for wolves, jays, blackbirds and squirrels. Now the killing price was twenty-five cents for a pair of woodchuck's ears and fifty cents for a crow's head.

BACKYARD TREASURE

Frank was very reticent as he hitched his horse to his buggy. For a long time he had been bragging about his secret blueberry patch, and he was anxious to be off before someone else discovered it.

We watched him drive away and then went into the house to get our buckets and large pail. We, too, were going blueberrying! We would go into the woods in back of Frank's barn, almost in sight of his house. All morning we gathered blueberries, pouring the contents of our smaller containers into the galvanized pail. At last it was filled, brimming with plump, juicy blueberries.

Late in the afternoon, Frank returned. He immediately drove over to our house and proudly displayed the six quarts of blueberries he had gathered. We never showed him the twelve-quart pail of blueberries sitting on our kitchen table awaiting the preserving kettle.

SHAKEY QUARTERS

The children at the Central School were excited. Now it doesn't take much to cause excitement as far as school routine is concerned, but this was a little out of the ordinary. The rope in the pulley was caught at the top of the flagpole above the roof of the school. There was much speculation and advice about how to untangle it. Finally, the custodian, Mr. Estes, offered a quarter to anyone who would climb the pole and release it. Herbert Deming, better known as Oopie, was the first to volunteer. All the school children and teachers watched as Oopie shinnied up the pole.

As he moved upward, the pole swayed back and forth amidst the oh-h-h and ah-h-h of the children and the final thunderous shout, "He did it!" Oopie was the hero of the day, and proudly collected his treasure of 25 cents which he fingered and then dropped into his pocket.

DEADLY PRIDE

(As told by Mrs. Thompson, Sunday School Superintendent)

Lily was a very attractive girl. She had been invited to go to the Valentine Ball with Ben, who was someone very special. All day she thought about the ball, and, as she ironed the yards of ruffle on the new blue dress she had just finished sewing, she hoped Ben would be pleased and that she indeed would be the belle of the ball.

It was about three o'clock in the afternoon. The thermometer had dropped suddenly and a strong wind blew out of the north. Lily became worried, and around four o'clock, she checked the thermometer again and saw that it hovered around zero. She dressed carefully, putting on her lovely new dress and piling her chestnut hair high on her head. She had a white woolen shawl which she wrapped around her shoulders. Hugging it to her, she stopped for a glimpse of herself in the long mirror. She turned this way and that admiring herself. Hearing a knock, she flew down the stairs and pulled open the door. There stood Ben with a big grin and admiring eyes which flattered Lily immensely. He handed her a Valentine box of candy and talked a few minutes with her family. Lily's mother insisted that she wear her warm coat, but Lily refused, wearing it on her arm instead.

After Ben had helped her into the buggy, he entreated her to put on her coat as it was very cold. Lily refused. Noticing Ben's worried expression, she smilingly told him that her pride would keep her warm. Besides, she didn't want to wrinkle her new dress. "Then let me cover your lap with my warm carriage robe," pleaded Ben. But again she refused.

As they drove along Lily was shaking with the cold and Ben tried many times to cover her but she pushed the robe away. After a while Lily said she felt warm and stopped shaking. She even hummed a little tune, then was quiet for the rest of the ride.

Upon arrival at the dance, Ben stepped down from the buggy and lifted his hand to help Lily. She did not move. It was then that Ben sadly realized that Lily had frozen to death.

THE GYPSY MOTH HUNTERS

Early every spring after the mud season, the town paid a gypsy moth crew to destroy the eggs of the moth. Each man carried a long bamboo fishing pole with a paint brush attached to the small end of it. He also carried a can of creosote. The men would walk along the town roads in pairs, one on either side of the road, looking for gypsy moth egg clusters on the trunk or underside of large limbs. When they found them they painted them with creosote.

They also had the task of searching for and destroying gooseberry and currant bushes. The owner of the land would be paid twenty-five cents a bush for each one destroyed. This was done because the currant and gooseberry bushes were hosts for the insect which caused the deadly White Pine Blister Rust.

Painting Gypsy Moth Nest

THE CLEANSING

Angelina Treetoad did a great deal of swearing on the school grounds. Her teacher, Miss Haliday, had spoken to her many times but Angelina had paid no attention. Finally Miss Haliday decided that she must do something very drastic in order to impress on the rest of the children that this behavior was unacceptable.

When the recess bell was rung, Miss Haliday lined all of the children up on either side of the school corridor, leaving only the sink with its pitcher-type hand pump in full view. She went to the sink and called Angelina to come and stand beside her. She slowly and deliberately filled the small basin with water, then took a bar of soap from the dish and whipped up frothy suds. She pick up a small glass standing on the shelf and put a small amount the soapy water into it. She then opened Angelina's mouth and poured the contents into it. Angelina immediately spit out the soapy water and rinsed out her mouth. Never again did the children hear her swear while on the playground.

EASY DOES IT

Nettie Bourne was a nag in most everyone's opinion. Her husband Lester was a very quiet, droll person. One day, when asked how he could live with his nagging wife, he answered, "Well, if wasn't for her, life would be awfully monotonous!"

Life is not Monotonous!

FRANCES, THE BLACK BEAUTY

George Lyons was a bachelor who lived in two houses about one thousand feet apart on Fuller Street. In the winter, he lived in the one-story house which had a barn and carriage shed in the rear. He kept his black driving horse named Frances in this barn.

In the summer, he lived in his attractive two-story brick house. Across the street, he had a barn and a drive-on platform scale which was used to weigh the hay stored on his property. Rube Braddock, his neighbor, used his horses and farm equipment to help George farm his land. Together they raised potatoes which were stored in the house cellar until sold. The rest of the land was used to raise hay that was stored in the two barns.

George's driving horse, Frances, had so much pep that it took George a while to devise a scheme by which Frances could be safely hitched to the light driving buggy. First George would hitch Frances to a heavy wagon and let her bolt a few clips around the hay field to get the pep out of her. Then Frances could be driven on a fast twenty-mile round trip to town on the driving buggy without so much as a backward glance.

George had a neighborhood bachelor friend named Woody who rode with him to town quite often. In good summer weather on Sundays, George and Woody would ride in the light wagon to Duxbury Beach and spend the day sitting on the beach watching the bathing beauties. As the sun was setting in the west, George and Woody gathered up their belongings and started homeward, reminiscing together about the events of the day.

George eventually sold his farm to a family from Kennebunkport, Maine, and, as Frances was part of the farm, this proud black beauty now became the property of someone equally as spirited, the young daughter, Margaret.

Margaret became a school teacher in Halifax, and was soon a familiar figure driving her jet black horse and shiny buggy to the Central School, which was just three miles away. For years, she rode in the buggy pulled by Frances every school day in all kind of weather.

During the school day Frances was boarded at the Colby's barn across from the church.

Frances served long and faithfully and when she was no longer able to make the trip, Margaret bought an automobile. Even though Frances lost the race to the automobile, Margaret never missed an opportunity to spend some time with a now rather aged black beauty. In time, illness and age brought a merciful sleep to Frances, the black beauty of Halifax.

LEW BROWN'S MELONS

Lew Brown loved to raise watermelons and took pride in watching them grow. The quality and flavor of his melons was well known to all with whom he so generously shared. The garden was well prepared. A mixture of poultry and cow manure was spaded under each hill which he planted after Memorial Day. Then, as the melon vines grew, he applied a liquid manure he called "garden tea."

When the melons were ripe and hung large and green on the vines, Lew Brown would pile a few into his wagon when he went to town on errands. He would give one to each of his business friends. They in turn would be happy to do favors for him such as give discounts on goods and tell helpful information. I remember we always kept a melon in a bucket in the well if we did not have ice.

When the sun was warm in the middle of the day, Lew would sit and read his mail and farm magazines in the shade of the tall maple tree that grew in the field by the road. If a neighbor or tramp walked or slowly drove by, he offered a cold piece of watermelon. Everyone, young or old, knew he could have a watermelon for the asking.

One day Lew went to his garden and was shocked and sick to discover that thoughtless, inconsiderate vandals had destroyed his large crop of watermelons. However, this did not dismay Lew and the next year he planted them closer to the house where he could keep an eye on them. This also allowed him to continue sharing his melons which he loved to do so well.

THE SANITATION ENGINEER
(As told by Neil Corneally)

Two neighbors were passing the time of day with Frank, the owner of a small country store. Frank was bragging about his cousin who had a very important position as Sanitation Engineer in the Health Department in Plymouth. The neighbors were very curious about Frank's cousin, so the next time they went to Plymouth they decided to look him up. They inquired about him at two or three places and then went to the Town Offices to inquire.

They were told that if they drove their buggy down the main street they would probably find him. They would recognize him because he would be dressed in a white uniform and he would be pushing a street cleaning hand cart.

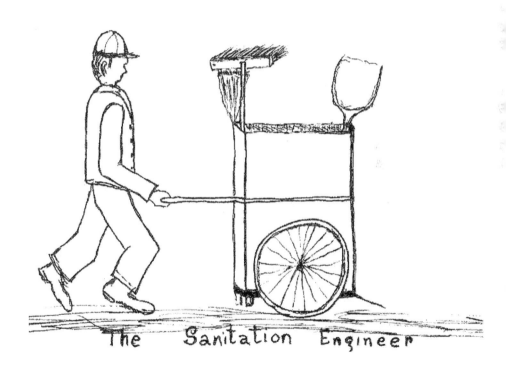

"ANY VANILLA EXTRACT TODAY?"

Roscoe was a familiar figure in this area. For many years he had been going from house to house peddling vanilla. His high nasal voice querying, "Any vanilla today?" was a trademark. These fine vanilla extracts were manufactured in Plympton and were prized by the fine cooks in the community.

When Roscoe died many people felt very sad. Roscoe was an old bachelor and did not have any family to mourn his passing. The village people decided to set their chores aside and attend the funeral services at the local church. Imagine their surprise to find the church already filled with other people who had felt the same way.

The young minister was new and was not acquainted with the community. As he looked out over his large audience, he was extremely nervous. He determined within himself that he would give a fine memorial and prayed with great earnestness that Roscoe's wife and children would be comforted by the loss of this beloved husband and father.

Everyone sat very still during this sober time. However, the young minister was never allowed to forget his mistake.

FINE EXAMPLE

(As told by Marshall Blackman)

We were riding in the farm wagon with Uncle Gus who had taken us into town while he did some errands. We rode over the dirt road, listening to the crunch of the wheels on the gravel and the steady clopping of the horse's hooves. It was a pleasant sound and we thought it would be a good time to ask our favorite uncle, who had been dubbed "storytelling Gus", to tell us a story.

He was most willing to oblige, and, holding the reins loosely in his hands, started spinning his yarn. He told us how people should get along together and said some animals he knew about had set a fine example. For instance, his neighbor had a raccoon and a woodchuck who had been sharing the same pen for over a year. They had never had any trouble between them. Why couldn't people be the same?

Uncle Gus had so impressed us that we asked him to drive us to the farm where these two animals were kept. He readily agreed, and at the right time, he turned into the long driveway that led to the neighbor's farm.

The two men exchanged pleasantries during which Gus asked if he might show the boys the two animals. We were walking to the pen where the two animals were kept, when Gus suddenly stopped short. We turned to look at him and noting his astonished expression, ran to the pen arriving just in time to see the raccoon finishing off the woodchuck.

47

THE BEAUTIFUL DOLL

Bill, the town's most eligible bachelor, had attended the Saturday night dance where he met a most charming and beautiful red-headed middle-aged widow. He became infatuated with her on sight, but he could not see her alone, as she had been escorted there by someone else.

As luck would have it, the next day after the church service, she was standing alone. Bill immediately asked her to go for a buggy ride and picnic. She was most agreeable and said she would pack a lunch and be ready at two o'clock.

At two o'clock sharp, Bill arrived with his black horse and shiny buggy. He helped her into the buggy and could not help admiring her red hair and rosy cheeks. They arrived at a most pleasant picnic site on a grassy slope beside a winding river. Bill stopped the buggy and helped her down. As she carried the picnic basket and settled under a large Hawthorn tree, he watered the horse and hitched him.

The afternoon passed all too quickly and they were getting ready to go home. Bill reached out his hand to help her get up but she moved quickly to get up by herself, catching her hair on the low branch of the Hawthorn tree. She moved her hands to free herself and as she did so her beautiful red wig was left hanging on the branch. Surprised and embarrassed she started to cry and, as she did so, the tears streaked her rouged cheeks.

Bill looked at her. All that was left of this beautiful doll were two blue eyes that looked pleadingly into his. Never hesitating, Bill took her into his arms and kissed her bald head while watching the red wig sway in the breeze.

FRESH MEADOW HAY

A half-century ago, thousands of acres of meadow grass grew in great, green arcs along the banks of the winding Winnetuxet River. It was a valuable natural resource, providing bedding for animals and insulation along the sills of the farmhouses to aid in keeping the floors warmer during the winter months. It was also used for insulating the great cakes of ice stored in the icehouses and sold in chunks during the summer months. Excelsior had not as yet been perfected, so manufacturers used meadow grass for packing material.

For years, Mr. Smith had harvested the meadow hay on Cedar Street. Each August, he would be seen driving his horse and hay wagon with haying tools to his large acreage along the river. All morning he would hand scythe the tall grass. At noon he watered and fed his horse and then ate his own lunch. After resting, he raked the cut meadow hay into piles and later drove his horse and wagon onto the swampy meadow to load. Since the meadow was filled with many boggy spots, the horse usually floundered into a bog hole and could not get free until help arrived from nearby neighbors.

Freeing a horse from a bog hole is not an easy task. Upon the arrival of his neighbor with another horse the situation was discussed. This might take some time. Usually a rope would be tied around the tail of Mr. Smith's horse and the other end of the rope attached to the whippletree (a horizontal wooden bar just in front of the plough) of the spare horse.

Tumbril Sledge to pull Meadow Hay across marsh Land

By this time several volunteers had arrived and with their help, together with the tremendous pulling by the other horse, Smith's horse was finally freed. After this was done, they helped load the remaining hay and returned to their respective farms.

This area today is still full of bog holes and enterprising people have tried to use heavy equipment to carry out some of their projects. However, after repeated miring of equipment they have abandoned the idea.

INVESTIGATION

Two ladies from the Boston Home Missionary Society rode the train to Halifax Depot where they rented a horse and buggy from Ed Dutton, the station master. They drove to South Street where they stopped at the home of Clarence Devitt to find out how to get to South Halifax. They told him that they had been sent down from Boston to investigate a complaint that they had received.

Mr. Devitt did not want a disparaging report to go back to Boston so he sent them to visit the Speakmans, the most refined family in that area. After this visit the ladies returned to Boston with a good report.

THE ESCAPADE
(a fact and fancy story)

After buggy driving twelve miles to reach the main street in Middleboro, I took out the horse-hitch weight and placed it at the edge of the sidewalk. I then fastened the snap unto the horse's bridle so the horse and buggy would be safely hitched at the side of the road while I did my errands.

As I came out of the store, there was a lot of excitement taking place in the area where I had left my horse and buggy. Moving quickly to the scene I acted like an innocent bystander in the growing crowd. I saw that another horse had broken loose and, with his carriage, had walked across the street and was rubbing noses with my horse. To complicate matters, his carriage was standing across the trolley tracks in the middle of the street. Down the hill came the trolley with the motorman madly clanging his bell in an effort to clear the tracks. The trolley car came to a screeching halt.

All of this commotion had attracted the foot policeman who was munching on a very large ice cream cone. Upon seeing the policeman approach, the carriage horse reared on his hind legs. As he did so, the policeman tripped over my horse's hitch line and fell on his ice cream. I thought I would have to become involved, but just then along came the carriage horse owner and led his horse away.

At this precise moment my horse became diverted by an inquisitive woman's straw hat and started chewing the flowers off of it. She screamed and moved to complain to the policeman. As she did so her hat pin pricked my horse's sensitive nose and he squealed and raised his head.

While all of this was happening, two policemen chanced along and had seen the whole escapade. They were laughing so hard that one of them, who was chewing a cut of tobacco, swallowed it and became sick.

No one noticed the trolley motorman's troubles. The trolley power pole had become unfastened from the overhead trolley wire and the trolley could not move. The passengers were getting off and demanding their fare back. As if this wasn't enough, someone, upon

51

seeing the flames and sparks at the trolley pole, had pulled the fire alarm. Down the street raced the fire engine with its clangity-clang-clang. This caused the excited horses tied along the street to pull and tug and squeal in a frenzy.

With the policemen so busy with the great traffic jam and total confusion which had been created, I decided that this was a good time to quietly lead my horse and buggy through a side alley and drive home. I had had enough excitement for one day.

DECISIONS

The farmer had a new hired man who was the best worker he had ever employed. One day, the farmer asked the hired man to sort out potatoes. When the hired man did not show up for dinner, the farmer went to the potato cellar in search of him. When he got there he found his hired man sitting on a wooden box holding a potato. "What is the matter?" inquired the farmer. "Why is it that you have sorted so few potatoes?"

The hired man looked up and replied, "I don't mind hard work but it is these decisions that I can't make."

DOCTORS CHARLES AND LOBDELL

In the early 1900's there were no telephones and the only way to contact a doctor was to write to him or have someone with a fast driving horse go and get him. Doctor Charles lived in Bryantville Center and he looked like Santa Claus. Everyone liked him and he was kind and faithful through all the years. I well remember the year so many people died with the flu and three of us in our family were very sick. Doctor Charles sat by my bed, played with a pull-string wooden horse, and quietly remarked, "We all have a little boy in us."

It was told that one time he could not get through to a sick family because the snow was too deep for his horse. The neighborhood men tramped a road through the snow and pulled him in the sleigh to save his strength.

Another doctor in our area was Doctor Lobdell, who was a veterinarian. He would say, "Yes, yes, pay me what you want." He was considered to be very good. Many farmers would have him check their health or the health of a member of the family when he was at the farm to treat an animal. He lived near Silver Lake, had a good fast driving horse, and was kept quite busy.

THE SECRET

In early times before the glass mirror was ever seen by those living in remote areas, a traveling salesman visited Gus. As they were looking and discussing the goods offered for sale, Gus told the salesman that he would pay a great deal if only he could have a picture of his beloved grandfather. The salesman thought quickly and fished into his bag bringing out a small mirror that he handed to Gus. Gus held the mirror before him for a long time and then said excitedly, "Yes, sir, this is indeed a fine picture of my beloved grandfather."

He immediately bought the mirror along with other supplies for his farm. As soon as the salesman left, Gus started to worry. He knew Biddy, his wife, would be extremely upset if she knew he had spent so much money for his grandfather's picture. After thinking about it, he decided to hide it under the hay mound in the barn.

Biddy, who always sat in her favorite rocking chair beside the kitchen window, had observed Gus' stealthy behavior as he went to the barn day after day at different times. Her suspicions were greatly aroused and, one day, she quietly followed him. She hid in the shadows and surreptitiously watched as Gus brought out a square object, which he lovingly held in his hands. He turned it one-way and then another and seemed fascinated by it. She could bear it no longer and sprang from her hiding place. Snatching the shiny object from his hands, she gazed for a long time at the reflection she saw there. Finally, she look incredulously at him and said, "Is this the hussy whose picture you have been hiding from me for this long time?"

FARMER BROWN MAKES HAY WHILE THE SUN SHINES

Congenial neighbors would team up to work together during haying time. A neighbor with a team of horses would usually do the mowing and help bring the cured hay into the barn. The neighbor with one horse would do the teddering, or the turning over of the hay to be cured with a pitchfork. Many times this was done with the help of the children. Haying had to be done when the weather was right, so the whole family cooperated. One child would drive the horse to rake up the hay while another would be on the wagon treading down and spreading as the hay was being forked by two farmers. Sometimes the housewife would bring down a nice cold drink of ginger water.

When the team of hay was brought into the barn, a large hayfork was often stuck into the load. Then the rope from the large hayfork went through a block above the loft into which the hay was to be hoisted. While the wagonload of hay waited inside the barn, another horse was hitched to a whippletree and led by someone. The farmer then stuck the fork into the hay load and the horse would pull away from the barn as the fork swung upward with its load of hay. When it reached the overhead block, the farmer would pull a trip rope to release the hay and it would fall onto the hay mound. Then the horse would return to the starting place, the farmer would pull the fork back to load again with his trip rope, and the process would be repeated.

In the meantime, the other farmer receiving the dropped hay in the hay mound would pitchfork the hay to the back corners, as it was needed. Usually a young boy would place it further back and tramp it under the eaves in order to store as much hay as possible.

Salt was sprinkled on each tier of hay to keep it from heating and the farm animals liked the taste of it. In this way, the hay could be harvested at each farm according to the terms previously arranged.

After the cultivated hay was harvested, the fresh meadow hay along the sides of the river was cut by hand scythe. It was then carried out by hand to the higher banks to be cured, and then carried home in the farm wagon. It was usually stored inside if there was room, but if not, it was stacked outside with a canvas over the top.

Many farms at this time raised corn and placed the husked ears in a corncrib to cure. Other farmers raised sweet corn to retail and then stacked the cornstalks in wigwam style to be fed to the cattle after milking. Often turnips, carrots, potatoes, and other vegetables normally raised for retail, but the leftovers or culls, were given to the cattle and poultry.

"ASK AND YE SHALL RECEIVE..."
(As told by my father)

A kindly minister who accepted chicken and surplus garden produce in lieu of financial gifts pastored the village church. At the weekly prayer meeting, his parishioners were encouraged to pray, believing that their prayers would be answered.

One day, as the pastor was walking along the village street, he met a well-dressed gentleman who was visiting friends. They stopped to talk for a while. Finally, the gentleman asked, "Why do you wear an alarm clock around your neck?"

"Because I have no watch," answered the pastor.

Without hesitation, the gentleman reached into his pocket and pulled out a beautiful gold watch. Placing it in his hand he handed it to the pastor and said, "God bless you, take mine."

SOUTH STREET BRIDGE

South Street Bridge, which crosses the Winnetuxet River, was once the boundary line of the Indian Purchase and the border of the town of Middleberry later known as Middleboro. In 1734, this land was incorporated as a part of Halifax.

Years ago the Fullers laid planks weighted with rocks on the riverbed and, in time, as these planks became water soaked and heavy, the stones could be removed. This solid base allowed teams of oxen and horse-drawn vehicles to cross during normal river flow that was usually less than two feet deep.

In 1741, a school was erected on the north side of the river within a short distance of this fording place. Because the river could not be crossed during winter and early spring freshets, school sessions took place during the summer months. A traveling schoolmaster who spent four months at each school in the town taught students.

In 1757, a bridge was built on this wading place and the material in the plank crossing was used.

From the time of its construction until the present time, this bridge has been a favorite meeting place for local people. This was especially true during the horse and buggy era when people from nearby would walk to the bridge to visit with neighbors and friends. On hot summer days, many would go for a refreshing swim.

Many times after the chores were finished, farmers would congregate on this bridge to fish. When twilight descended they would light a lantern and, holding it by a rope, would drop it close to the river's surface to attract hornpout. Usually they returned home with a full pail of hornpout that were dressed off and put on ice for a neighborhood fish fry the following day.

Winnetuxet River

In late winter and early spring the water would rise two feet or more, flooding the road and covering the bridge. Sometimes the river was so full of floating ice that the horses would have their legs cut and bleeding by the time they had crossed. Halifax later voted to raise the height of the road and the bridge.

There is a worn path beside the bridge that leads to a flat launching area. It is the same site used long ago to water horses and to launch boats and canoes. Today, would-be Tom Sawyers still pole their rafts along with the current while they fish and dream of bygone days.

THE COURTSHIP OF MISS JONES

Miss Jones was our teacher in the second-story room that faced west in the grammar school in Halifax. Her home was in Bridgewater, so throughout the week she boarded at Miss Jewett's Boarding House that was within easy walking distance from the school. Her knight-in-shining-armor was Earl Gummow, a dairyman whose farm was west of the school at Furnace Pond.

This late Friday afternoon was especially bright. It had stopped snowing and the sun had just come out, causing everything to sparkle and glisten. As was her custom, she always held a reading class at the last period every Friday. Miss Jones planned it this way so that the teacher across the hall could dismiss us and allow Miss Jones to leave a bit early. The room was very still and we could hear the big clock ticking away the time. We would glance surreptitiously at Miss Jones over the tops of our books and enjoy watching her watch the clock.

Suddenly from the west, we heard the tinkling of sleigh bells, which grew louder and clearer as they came nearer. Miss Jones blushed shyly as the children watched out of the window. We heard the crunching of the runners as they moved over the snow and the sharp melodic ring of the bells. We could no longer sit quietly, so we stretched our necks and rose as one to look out of the window. We saw a frisky black driving horse pulling a black and red sleigh coming into the schoolyard. Miss Jones gathered her things and with a quick, "Goodnight, boys and girls," flew down the steps and into the sleigh.

It was such a beautiful picture as they drove away that it will remain one of my very pleasant memories.

THE DAY THE LIGHTNING STRUCK

It was a very hot day in July. The neighbors had just helped Mr. Speakman pull all of his hay into the barn. Suddenly it began to pour, and everyone got very wet going home.

Lewis Brown was one of those who had been helping. He was just putting on dry clothes when a very brilliant, blinding flash of lightning, followed by the sound of a terrific roll of thunder, struck the corner of the hay barn. The barn seemed to explode and the roof burst into flames. The lightning bolt jumped to the flagpole in front of the barn and killed the cow that was chained to it.

The sound of all this, together with the flames and smoke, attracted horse-drawn vehicles with fire-fighting tools from many miles around. All the neighbors formed a chain of hands from the well to the men on the roof, and pails of water were emptied onto the igniting sparks and burning debris.

To replace the destroyed structure, Dave Briggs and neighbors built a smaller barn, and a separate hay barn was put up in the backfield in sight of the icehouse. One Fourth of July someone set fire to the hay barn and that was the end of it. That someone was obviously not a good neighbor.

SCHOOL BARGE

At the time of this story, I was a kid living in South Halifax. New neighbors had moved into the brown-shingled house on Wood Street and we were all very curious to learn more about them. One day we walked very, very slowly past Mr. Anderson's house and since he was out getting a wheelbarrow load of wood, he saw us and asked us if we would like a fresh doughnut and a glass of milk. We accepted the invitation with alacrity. Mr. Anderson had just retired as a streetcar conductor in the city of Boston. In anticipation of his retirement, he had spent a great deal of time reading about different places in the area and had reached the conclusion that country living was something, which he and his wife, Elsie, would enjoy. They admitted that they liked the country but they missed the hustle and bustle of the city and found the shriek of the blue jay and the early crowing of a neighbor's rooster as disturbing as some of the city noises.

In time, the Andersons fit into the routine of country life and were very active in the community. Mrs. Anderson was extremely involved at the local church and taught a large class of adolescent girls.

As the years went by, Mr. Anderson felt that he would have to supplement his pension. Upon making inquiries, he learned that the school barge contract was up for bids and he immediately secured the necessary papers. He was awarded the contract because he was the lowest bidder.

The summer months were spent purchasing the necessary equipment for his new endeavor. It was relatively easy to acquire a used school barge and pang, but buying a team of horses proved to be too expensive. After considerable searching, Mr. Anderson found a large chestnut horse, which the children named Elephant, and a smaller non-descript white horse, dubbed Camel. Mr. Anderson would not be using both horses all of the time but would need them both during the long winter months and the early spring mud season.

In September, Mr. Anderson, our new barge driver, stopped at our house to pick up Dick, Betty and me. Along the route, boys and girls mounted the back steps and walked along the narrow aisle to find a vacant seat on the side.

Perhaps the best time of year for riding the school barge was during the autumn. The days were usually cool and crisp and the trees were bright with their fall colors. One beautiful October day, when the color was at its peak, the children left the barge and went through the woodland paths gathering armfuls of colored leaves. They jumped back into the barge and immediately started decorating. Colorful leaves hung from the roof and were stuck into the backs of the seats. When all of the leaves had been placed in all kinds of positions, the children threw themselves onto their seats and sang loudly and joyfully all the way to school. However, their happiness was short-lived, because a few days later some of the children came down with very severe cases of poison ivy.

During the winter months, the children rode to school on Mr. Anderson's pung (a sleigh with a boxlike body). Usually the floor was spread with sweet smelling hay and a few robes were available for the children to use. When it was sub-zero weather, some of the children brought a heated brick or soapstone wrapped in newspaper to be placed at their feet once they climbed onto the pung. When everyone who could reach the warmth of the package was settled, someone would grab a blanket and the children would pull it up around their chins with bland grins.

Once my brother's brick was too hot and soon the paper started to smolder. I noticed it just in time and quickly threw it out of the pung.

When the weather was not too cold, some of the children would jump off and run along with the pung. This helped to keep them warm for we had a three-mile ride to school. When they became winded, they would jump back onto the pung and huddle together under the robes.

During the months of March and April, school usually closed because of the very muddy roads. When the roads had dried out sufficiently to allow travel, school would reopen. We were always glad to see Mr. Anderson driving Elephant and Camel down the road.

As the horses plodded along, some of the boys and girls would jump off the barge and run through connecting wood roads, then meet up with the barge again. In late spring, the children would gather wildflowers as they ran through the woodland roads and would proudly present them to their teachers.

Mr. Anderson was kind and the children loved and respected him. Often, as the horses plodded along, the children would plead with him to make them run faster. He always tried to oblige but they only trotted a little ways and then continued their slow monotonous plodding.

The combustion engine finally replaced the barge. This made transportation faster, more comfortable and more efficient. However, I cannot think of any happening on the school bus that has filled me with more nostalgia than those events, which occurred in my childhood while riding the barge drawn by Elephant and Camel.

School Barge

CITY AND STATE WARDS

City and State wards were children who were taken in by Halifax families to supplement their family income. Later, many of them became a credit to the town of Halifax. With few exceptions, these children became very good citizens and several of them grew up and returned here to marry into local families. In some cases, they even became town officials.

Several children, after having lived in Halifax for a few years, went to Boston for the purpose of finding their own parents. After visiting their parents, they were much happier at their foster parents' home. In some cases, the foster parents boarded them when they became older. Some foster parents willed their farms to them. In one case, after the foster mother died, the foster father married the widowed mother of his ward children.

The children of the town always treated these ward children as friends even though many of them were just a wee bit envious of their new clothes, which were so much nicer than what their own parents could afford. I feel Halifax performed a great human service during this period of history.

A GRAVE PROBLEM

I am very much interested in dowsing and sometimes attend the American Society of Dowsers Convention that is held each fall in Danville, Vermont. A few years ago, a friend, Steve Smith, attended one of these sessions with me and upon returning home worked diligently at the art and became a very good dowser.

One day, Police Chief Ramsey of Alexandria, New Hampshire telephoned Smith and asked him to meet him at the Riverside Cemetery to assist in a grave-digging project. Smith got into his Jeep and drove down to the cemetery to find Ramsey greatly perplexed. He had to dig a new grave for a Mrs. Smith (no relation) but he did not know where the husband was buried. There were no records showing the grave location and the only thing on the plot was a headstone. "Where, oh, where, shall I dig without hitting the other grave?" lamented Ramsey.

Steve Smith suggested that perhaps he could help by dowsing. Ramsey looked at him in disbelief and disdainfully suggested that dowsing was a lot of "hogwash." Nonetheless, there seemed no other solution and he finally agreed to let Smith try. Cutting a Y branch from a nearby tree, Smith stripped off the leaves and proceeded to dowse around the gravestone. Sure enough, the stick responded and he was able to mark out the location and size of the cement vault buried below. Now came the test! Cautiously Ramsey dug the new grave with his backhoe—two feet away and beside the husband's vault.

Smith jumped into the new grave to hand dig and square out the site and while digging he pulled out a broken tree root which was two feet long with a fresh break on one end and an old break on the other. Upon investigation, he found that it had been broken when the husband's grave had been dug.

Ramsey was amazed and reluctantly declared that perhaps dowsing really did work. In any event, time after time when Ramsey was digging a well for a neighbor and struck a dry hole, he would telephone Smith to come down and dowse for water and each time the well was successful. Today Ramsey is a real believer in dowsing and recommends it to everyone.

UNCLE GUS GOES TO CHURCH

Uncle Gus and Aunt Laura lived up in the hills near Mt. Cardigan three miles from the nearest village that was located in the flats called Alexandria. The people who lived in the flats felt that they were above the people who lived in the hills and the mountain people looked down on those who lived in the flats. However, they needed each other and there was good fellowship in spite of the prejudices.

Uncle Gus and Aunt Laura loved people and at the drop of a hat would leave the farm work and get out into society to see what was going on. They had a good horse and buggy and a rain shield ready when needed. Often it would be fair when they left home and when they got to the village, because of the change in elevation, it might be raining.

They looked forward to attending the village church on Sundays. This gave them the opportunity to greet friends whom they had met at the Grange and other local residents. Usually, while at church, someone would invite them for dinner and fellowship. The afternoon passed pleasantly and when the time came for each family to do their chores, Uncle Gus would hitch up the wagon and head home. Before leaving, he would pull out a comb of wild bee honey from beneath the seat of the buggy and present it as a token of his appreciation. His stay was prolonged for a few minutes while he went into great detail as to how he gathered the honey from a bee tree across the street.

The horse needed no encouragement to get home quickly and soon he was in his own stall where he could hear the friendly sounds of the other animals and fowl that made up the barnyard.

As for Uncle Gus and Aunt Laura, when the evening chores were finished and they had eaten a light supper, they were ready to retire and dream of the happy events of the day.

Alexandria, N.H.

HBrown

THE GHOST OF THE SEA CAPTAIN
(A true story as told to me by Dr. Chase)

One Friday I was visiting with my wife, who was in the hospital with pneumonia. Her attending physician, Dr. Chase, came into the room. During her visit, we talked about many different things and she was particularly interested in my dowsing experiences. She said she would like to find the old underground pipeline that ran from her pond to the barn. Her married daughter, Ellen, was a good dowser and used a natural forked stick to find water. I explained that she could also find water or even underground pipes by walking over them with two L shaped metal rods. They should be held apart, one in each hand, in a parallel position. If either was over the pipe or water, they would cross over one another in an X formation or they would spread apart in opposite directions.

As I entered the hospital lounge the following Monday afternoon, Dr. Chase approached me and asked if I would have time to come to her office as she had something important to discuss with me. I immediately went to her office and she told me the following story.

Her daughter Ellen and her husband had gone to Nantucket Island over the weekend. Upon returning, she told her mother the story, which she was sure, would be of great interest to me.

As Ellen and her husband boarded the ferry for Nantucket, Ellen became extremely apprehensive about the trip and confided her fears to her husband. He did not take them very seriously. Nonetheless, Ellen had a strong premonition that not all was well and she was greatly disquieted.

After docking at Nantucket, they went to the Captain's House where they had made reservations. They spent the day touring the beautiful island and visiting the many shops. Much later, they returned to the Captain's House and immediately went to their room. They were very much impressed with the Colonial furnishings and especially liked the brass bed. After they had been in the room a while, Ellen had a strange foreboding.

As the night wore on, she was very restless. It seemed that every time she moved to the side of the bed she was immediately repulsed as if by an unseen force. Suddenly she was aware of the apparition of a sea captain standing at the foot of the bed. She felt mesmerized. It seemed to her as if the sea captain was trying to tell her something and she gathered that some sort of a tragedy had taken place in this room. She got the feeling that it occurred on the side of the bed from which she had been repulsed and had something to do with the closet on that side of the room.

In the meantime, a strange feeling awakened her husband, and when he snapped on the lights, the apparition vanished.

They were both fully awake by now and discussed the experience at length. Ellen was very upset but she suddenly became very curious about the whole episode and determined that she was going to solve it. She remembered her mother talking about dowsing with metal rods to find out different kinds of information.

She raced to the closet, took out two wire coat hangers, and bent them in an L shape. She held them over the bed where she had seemed to be repelled and there was an immediate strong reaction from the rods. She approached the closet and again received a strong reaction. This confirmed her belief that a tragedy had taken place in this room.

Ellen and her husband got very little sleep and the next morning checked out of the Captain's House. Even so, she wanted to return and see if she could solve the mystery of the captain's ghost at another time but could never get up enough courage to do so.

THE DAY THE GYPSIES CAME TO TOWN

It was a bright summer morning in our little town when the enchanting sounds of strange music floated through the air. We listened and soon the music sounded nearer and nearer. Around the bend of the main street appeared a brightly painted wagon with designs of flowers all over the enclosed body and with windows on either side. It was drawn by a pair of glossy black horses whose harnesses were decorated with shiny brass fittings, tassels and tingling bells. The horses pranced as if dancing to the beat of the music and the wagon wheels made a pleasant chucking sound in the background.

The wagon was driven by the father and chief of the caravan of three other wagons. He was dressed in a brightly colored uniform trimmed with gold braid and on the front seat with him was his portly, jolly wife gaily dressed as a fortuneteller. Between them stood their costumed pet monkey shaking a small tambourine. Inside the wagon were their curious children peeking out of the open windows to take in the sights.

As the wagon passed by, we saw that a platform enclosed by a small rail had been built at the rear, and sitting on a stool, was an older boy dressed as a pirate with a large gold earring dangling from one ear. He played his violin as his attractive sister walked on the road behind dancing and twirling her flared skirt as she beat time with her tambourines.

A pair of chestnut horses drew the second gaily-decorated enclosed wagon with harness finery on them also. In the driver's seat were two people with a performing dog proudly seated between them. The wagon had a hinged side, which was let down to become a stage.

The third wagon was a tinker shop and store. This wagon was drawn by a pair of dapple-gray horses and driven by a skilled tinker with his wife and child beside him.

The fourth and last wagon was a blacksmith and repair shop and was drawn by an odd pair of horses driven by the blacksmith and his son. At the rear of the wagon, three horses were attached with hitch ropes. These horses would be used for horse-trading.

As the caravan moved through the countryside and town on the way to their encampment, the local children and young people left their chores and followed them. Families decided to declare a holiday and hitched up their wagons. They loaded any pots and pans that needed mending by the tinker and any tools that could be repaired by the blacksmith. They also brought along any horse that needed new shoes. Then, with their families, they followed the caravan to its destination.

The caravan paraded along the main street of the town and turned into the amusement park field where there was a brook, a grove and ample facilities to take care of their own needs as well as those of their animals. They formed a large half circle with their wagons and, after caring for the horses, put them in a corral at the side rear of the field, where farmers could look them over and make trades.

In the meantime, the half circle of wagons was suddenly transformed into an entertainment center. Even though there were no telephones, news of the arrival of the gypsies had spread rapidly and soon a large crowd gathered and the road was crowded with wagons and buggies waiting their turn to enter the grounds.

At last it was time to start the performances. Suddenly, as if by magic, the encampment became a gala affair. The children gathered to watch the puppet shows and the young people crowded around the stage where they listened to the vibrant music of the accordion, violin and tambourines. Quietly a little ways off a gypsy fortuneteller was doing a brisk business.

While their family was being entertained, some of the men had gone to the blacksmith's wagon to have their tools repaired while others went to the corral to barter for a better horse. Most of them, however, joined their families around the wagons enjoying the festivities there.

Meanwhile, the women went to the tinker's wagon where they had their pots and pans repaired or bought new ones. They also bought trinkets, ribbons, buttons and other small items. Their faces glowed with happiness when they purchased the special refreshments and candies offered for sale. It was a great luxury!

In the meantime, wherever the crowd gathered to be entertained or to do business, the organ grinder with his performing dog roamed among them. After the act, a costumed monkey went around with his tin cup soliciting donations.

By mid-afternoon, a siesta was declared and everyone was invited to return for the evening's entertainment. This gave the gypsies an opportunity to eat and relax while the families returned home to do their chores, which, by the way, were completed in record time.

At dusk, the street was again thronged with people returning to the encampment. Even grand ma and pa decided they could stay up later than usual. Upon entering the grounds, they found that the gypsies had spent considerable time getting ready for them. The wagons were decorated with colorful lanterns and a large campfire was burning brightly in front of the half circle of wagons. Flaming torches were placed along the outside area providing an exciting background. Soon, the haunting music of the different instruments filled the air and there was much singing and dancing. After a period of fun and merrymaking, the evening was ended and the crowd dispersed to return to their homes.

The next morning, long before the villagers were awake, the gypsy caravan was well on its way to another town. For weeks and perhaps months, the people of the town talked about this happy event and looked forward to the return of the gypsies.

Made in the USA
Middletown, DE
03 November 2017